Roly-Poly Prole

Story by **Elizabeth Javidan**
Illustrations by **Mary Barrows**

BELLE ISLE BOOKS
www.belleislebooks.com

ISBN: 978-1-953021-24-3
LCCN: 2021911800

Designed by Michael Hardison
Project managed by Christina Kann

Printed in the United States of America

Published by
Belle Isle Books (an imprint of Brandylane Publishers, Inc.)
5 S. 1st Street
Richmond, Virginia 23219

BELLE ISLE BOOKS
www.belleislebooks.com

belleislebooks.com | brandylanepublishers.com

To my children,
who remind me every day
what it is to love books
and to be loved back.

And to my husband,
who supports and inspires me
as only a fellow artist could.

My heart is full,
and you are my reasons why.

Roly-Poly Prole was quite a shy fellow.
He kept his head down and never said, "Hello."
Roly-Poly Prole was a humble bug, too.
With whatever he had, he simply made do.
He worked in the factory like all other Proles,
making weapons for cheap to fight "the great foe."

When Roly-Poly Prole was nervous or scared,
he'd curl up and pretend that he wasn't there.
He would coil up so tight in a small, sturdy ball,
so little and plain, no one saw him at all.
This was Roly-Poly's most treasured trick.
He tried to never catch the eyes of the Ticks.

The Ticks were the leaders, and every Prole knew,
because of the Ticks, the Proles' lives were blue.
Every night, the same thing would happen:
the TVs would turn on, and the Proles' hearts would sadden.
Videos would play before the Proles' eyes;
the daily news was propaganda and lies.
The Ticks would appear on the screens, gross and bulky,
leaving the Proles feeling frightened and sulky.
The Ticks gnashed their teeth and declared, "We are ONE!
Anyone who thinks differently will be shunned."

The biggest tick, Tick Acarus the Third,
stood behind the podium to make his voice heard.
"Our ancestors stood back as society fell.
They left us nothing to eat and no place to dwell.
To all who live, feel, breathe, and crawl,
the only way to stand is never to fall.
Keep your head down, and do not make trouble,
or the Bee Guards will arrive at your home on the double.
They will take you away; they'll lock you behind bars.
They will not treat you well; they'll leave you with scars.
Don't try to speak up. Listen to my voice!
Obeying these commands is your ONLY choice.
For your sake, we keep most of your earnings
to stop you from buying unnecessary things.
You have it made! Your life is easy!
We know what to do when you're unsure or queasy!
Where should you work? How should you survive?
We've solved these problems so that you can thrive.
We will think for you, so never forget
that Tick Acarus the Third understands you the best.
I've always been driven, and so I became
the most powerful leader in the world without shame."
Then he would puff out his chest, so swollen and large,
to show he was the biggest; he was in charge.

After the speech, the TVs would then play
the Ticks' favorite show, "The Trial of the Day."
In this program, a Roly-Poly was put on trial
for a crime they hadn't done, something quite vile.
The Bee Guards would cuff a Prole shaking with fear,
who, despite their strength, could not stop their tears.
"This Prole is a criminal!" Acarus would shout.
"They plotted against us! They have to be taken out!"
These images were enough to keep the Proles at bay,
for no Roly-Poly wanted to see their last day.
So Roly-Poly Prole lived his days quite plainly,
keeping to himself, trying to live sanely.

One day in the city, as he walked along, somber,
he heard a child crying, and slowly he wandered
toward the youngster who was making the sound—
a sound that he knew was the saddest around.
He walked down the sidewalk and knelt next to the child.
"What is wrong?" he asked, keeping his voice mild.
"They took my mother," the young girl replied.
"I don't know where she is, and I'm hungry," she cried.
Roly-Poly Prole wanted to curl into a ball,
forget what he'd heard, the crying and all.
But something inside the little child's eyes
told Roly-Poly Prole it was time to arise.
The Roly-Poly child had not curled into a ball;
She felt and she cried, sitting next to that wall.
If this Roly-Poly child had the courage to weep,
despite being warned to never make a peep,
then Roly-Poly Prole could be strong and brave.
This courageous child had shown him the way.

Roly-Poly Prole was a nice fellow to meet.
He took the girl home and gave her something to eat.
She gratefully ate what little food he had.
Then she fell right asleep, clearly feeling less sad.
As she peacefully slept, Roly-Poly watched her breathe,
and he began thinking, "How can someone be
so ruthless and selfish, to drain others so?"
Enough was enough; the Ticks had to go.
He kissed the girl on the head and then left a note
with the name of a neighbor who'd keep her afloat.
Roly-Poly Prole recalled friends and neighbors
he saw every day, exhausted from labor.
"They will help me; of this, I am sure.
This way of life simply cannot endure.
Who wants to go hungry or feel left without hope?
I am not the only one at the end of their rope."

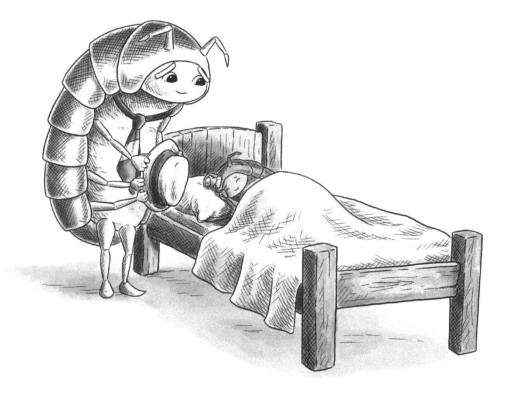

In the dark of the night, with no moon in sight,
he went out to discuss the Roly-Poly plight.
"If you want a change," Roly-Poly Prole said,
"meet me at midnight in the factory's toolshed."

Roly-Poly Prole waited in that shed with no heat
and was delighted at the sound of shuffling feet.
"They are here! They are ready! We will do this together!"
He turned on a light to see who had gathered.
Roly-Poly Prole began to feel truly brave
surrounded by friends, all these lives they would save.
"My dearest friends," he began, whispering quietly,
"we must do something to save this society.
We must come together to fight this injustice!
We must take the power away from Acarus
And the other Ticks, who drain us of life.
Together, we can handle this strife.
Our upcoming battle may need a few Proles
to risk their lives, so we can reach our goal.
The present is terrible, and no child should feel
that life can't be beautiful, that love can't be real.
For them, we will fight the great fight that awaits;
for them, no sacrifice is too great.
Roly-Polies, stand proud! Be not afraid;
we will put a stop to the Ticks' charade.
We will no longer accept what has been planned for us!
Gather your arms, and let's storm their fortress!"

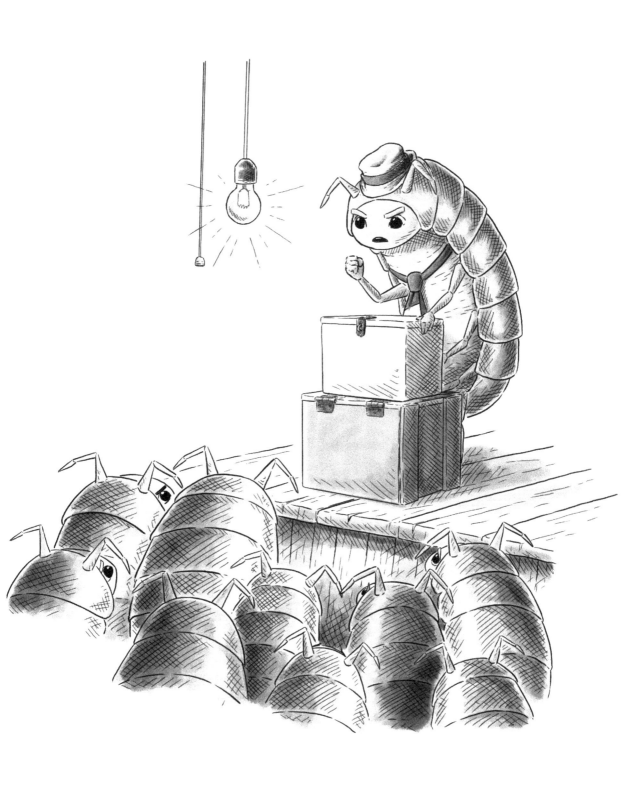

A ripple of cheers, as quiet as can be,
went through the crowd like the rustle of leaves.
The energy was strong; the timing was right.
It was the Proles' turn to bring on the fight.
The Roly-Polies boldly created their army
to finally take down the ruling Tick party.

Roly-Poly Prole took the lead to settle the score,
and he marched with a thousand against forty-four.
The Bee Guards were surprised when the Roly-Polies came;
they were sure that Bee strength would stop the Proles' aim.
The Bee Guards didn't know that their stingers couldn't stop
what had been set in motion by the Roly-Poly plot.
The Proles smoked the Bees into a peaceful, deep sleep
and stormed the Ticks' rooms in one silent sweep.

All forty-four Ticks slept in the same room;
the smell they produced caused the thickest of fumes.
The stench reeked of sadness and despair;
how could anyone sleep with that guilt in the air?

Roly-Poly Prole had outlined their goal:
to rope the Ticks 'round the tummies and take back control.
First, the Roly-Polies quietly curled into balls,
a defensive move that would now save them all.
Next, the Roly-Polies did what they do best:
they rolled silently past the Ticks' heaving chests.

They effortlessly captured all forty-four beasts
and marched them to the courthouse for a new brief.
All the Roly-Poly Proles were invited to attend.
They must choose a new leader to quickly ascend.

"My dearest Ticks," Roly-Poly Prole said into the mic,
"you have been brought here by those you dislike.
We Roly-Polies have reached a decision:
you all will star in the best show on television.
For years, the Roly-Polies have served under your rule.
We have listened to your lies, your most useful tool.
These lies kept us constantly scared and tired,
our children uneducated, and the people with no desire
to strive for a better life, no drive to achieve more.
But that ends today; we will even the score.
You will complete all our wishes; we have only three.

The first is to set all Roly-Polies free
from the jail where you kept them on charges of treason.
The second is to confess your lies to completion.
The third—you'll serve the same sentences you gave
innocent Roly-Polies. May you be just as brave.

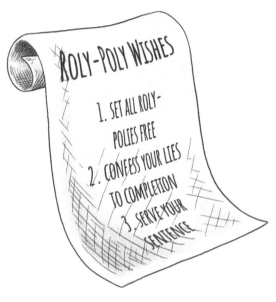

The Ticks looked at one another, taken aback.
How did this happen? Where had they slacked?
Acarus the Third scowled at the other Ticks.
What had they done wrong? What should they have fixed?

"Do you wish to object?" Roly-Poly Prole probed.
"Do you wish to beg for a new chance? For hope?"
"What good would it do?" Tick Acarus responded.
"You all have won; we are being discarded,
the Ticks who cared for you. You say it wasn't enough.
You all don't care that our lives, too, were tough.
Roly-Poly Prole, I leave you with this:
being a good leader means denying oneself bliss."
Roly-Poly Prole no longer felt yellow.
With one final glance, he gave a loud bellow:
"Let our wishes commence!" he valiantly declared.
He glared at the Ticks with an unfeeling stare.

The Roly-Polies' first wish was easy to complete;
Tick Acarus opened the jail doors in defeat.
The captured Roly-Polies could not believe their eyes
when their cell doors opened; what a surprise!
They fled the jail as fast as could be,
back to their loved ones, who were no longer wary.

The Roly-Polies' second wish took much more time.
The Ticks had a long list of confessions of crimes.
Once the Ticks had spilled their darkest of secrets,
they apologized for this long list of selfish grievances.

The third wish was completed with the help of the Bees,
who, when awakened from their sleep, completely agreed
to help the Roly-Polies by jailing the Ticks;
they'd have a second chance if they helped with the fix.
The Bee Guards handcuffed all forty-four Ticks
and led them away as they snarled and hissed.

Once the Ticks were sentenced and the celebrations subsided,
the Roly-Polies came together and quickly united.
They distributed the food that the Ticks had hoarded,
and for six months solid, the Roly-Polies were reported
to be content in their peaceful slumbers at night.
They no longer worried or suffered from fright.

The Bee Guards were now simply called "the Bees."
They enjoyed their new lives and felt quite at ease.
The Roly-Polies called their land "the Garden."
They felt that their hearts were no longer hardened.
The factories stopped production, and the skies that were gray
now shone bright blue under the sun's warming rays.
Trees and flowers blossomed; grim sadness was no more.
Hope was starting to feel genuinely restored.

After six months, the Roly-Polies held an election
and created some rules with specific subsections.
Roly-Poly Prole was unanimously elected
President of the Roly-Polies. The word "Prole" was ejected.

President
of the Roly Polies

☑ Roly-Poly

☐ Bee Guard #5

☐ Winston

Official Ballot

"My friends," Roly-Poly started his first speech,
"we will always live together in harmony and peace.
"For now, in such times, when the world feels renewed, we
will build a great nation on what's fair and true.
We will help one another and never be scared
to let our voices be heard and our thoughts be shared.
Every Roly-Poly has the right to love and happiness,
a place to call their own, and a warm bed in which to rest.
From now on, the Garden will belong to us all.
We cannot—we will not—let our loved ones fall.
Each Roly-Poly child will receive an education
and a career, so they will excel in this new nation.
It is all of our duties to make our country succeed
with Roly-Poly hard work and love for all who need."

Roly-Poly Leader was not shy anymore;
he always said, "Hello"—it was no longer a chore.
Roly-Poly Leader was still humble, too,
and under his leadership, the whole Garden grew.

About the Author

Elizabeth Javidan is a teacher-turned-author who loves books so much, she decided to write one. An award-winning newspaper columnist and avid book listener, Javidan has culminated her passion for equal rights, twentieth-century dystopian novels, and rhythmic poetry into her debut children's classic, *Roly-Poly Prole*. After encountering dozens of stories about life, hardship, and what it means to never give up on a dream of happiness, Javidan wanted to honor and congratulate those who, like her character, challenged what they knew was wrong and chose to persevere. In her "spare time," Javidan enjoys cooking, exercising, drinking copious amounts of coffee, and keeping up with her really, really cool kids.

About the Illustrator

Mary Barrows is a freelance illustrator from Maryland with a love of fantasy stories and creatures. Since she was old enough to hold a crayon, she has been drawing pictures of her favorite stories, and she has not stopped yet. Mary works both digitally and traditionally and uses a variety of mediums in her work including gouache, ink, watercolor, and colored pencil. To contact, visit www.marybarrows.wordpress.com or email at marybarrowsillustration@gmail.com

CPSIA information can be obtained
at www.ICGtesting.com
Printed in the USA
BVHW091214231121
622346BV00021B/1076